DEATH ON TOP

A MOUNTAIN MYSTERY UNCOVERED

AAYUSHI JINDAL

Made with ♥ on the Notion Press Platform
www.notionpress.com

Contents

ONE

The Climb Begins

Jack had been doing this for years, but each day was different. The climb was never easy but it was always worth it. As he climbed the steep trail to the summit, he felt a sense of freedom and peace that he had found nowhere else.

He had just reached a particularly challenging part of the trail when he heard a rumbling sound in the distance. Jack stops in his tracks trying to identify the source of the sound. After a few moments, he realized that it was a call for help. Without hesitation, Jack picked up his pace and started running towards the voice.

As he neared the source of the noise, Jack saw a group of hikers standing around a woman lying on the ground. She was unconscious and it was obvious that she had fallen from a great height. Jack recognized the woman as he had seen earlier on the trail, but he did not know her name.

"Are you okay?" he asked, as he ran towards the group of hikers.

"No, we need help," said one of them. "She fell off the side of the mountain. We don't know what to do."

Jack knew what he had to do. He had seen all this before. He had trained for it, and he was the only one who had the skill to do it. He had to fix the body, and he had to do it fast.

"I'll take care of that," he said, as he pulled out his climbing gear. "All of you need to be here."

Jack acted quickly, securing himself to the mountainside with his rope and pulling the woman's body down to the ledge. She was still alive, but barely. Jack checked her pulse and breathing and then carefully secured her in his harness before starting the climb.

As they near the top, Jack hears the woman moan in pain. He knew that if she was going to make it he would have to help her fast. When they finally reach the summit, Jack immediately calls for a helicopter to take the woman to the hospital.

As soon as he sees the helicopter take off, Jack knows he's made a difference. He had saved a life, and that was what mattered most. He also knew that this was just the beginning. He spent the rest of the day recovering the bodies, but it was the start of something big.

TWO

FIRST CLUE

After rescuing the hiker, Jack knew he needed to take a break. He sat down on a large boulder near the summit and breathed deeply, feeling the cool mountain air fill his lungs. As he sat there, he saw a group of travelers coming up the trail, looking tired and disheveled.

"Hey, do you know anything about the lady that was rescued?" one of the hikers asked as they reached Jack.

"I was the one who saved her," replied Jack.

The hikers were surprised and grateful, and thanked Jack for his heroism. While they were talking, Jack noticed a woman in the group who was studying him intently. There was a serious expression on her face, and Jack could tell that she had something on her mind.

"Can I help you with something?" he asked her.

The lady hesitated for a moment before speaking. "I don't mean to nitpick, but I hear you recover bodies from mountains. Is that true?"

Jack nodded. "Yeah, it is. It's a tough job, but someone's gotta do it."

The woman looked at the ground, seemingly lost in thought. "I know this may sound crazy, but I think I might know something about a body that was recovered a few years back. It was a suicide, and it happened on this mountain."

Jack got interested. "Do you have more information about this?"

The woman nodded. "I'm a reporter, and I'm investigating the story. I think there's more to this than just a simple suicide. There were some unusual circumstances surrounding the death, and I believe someone may have been involved."

Jack got interested. He had heard rumors about a mysterious death on the mountain, but had never been able to confirm them. "What can I do to help?"

The woman smiled, relieved that Jack was willing to listen. "I need someone who knows the mountain, someone who can help me navigate the terrain and find any clues that might still be there. Will you help me?"

Jack considered his request for a moment. He had recovered many bodies over the years, but he had never been involved in a mystery like this. It was risky, but it was also an opportunity to make a difference.

"I'll help you," he said, at last. "But we need to be careful. This mountain is unforgiving, and we don't know what might find us."

The woman nodded, grateful for Jack's willingness to help. As they were getting ready to leave on their journey, Jack couldn't help but feel a sense of excitement. They didn't know what they would find, but they were sure it was going to be a journey like nothing they've ever been on before.

THREE

First Clue Revealed

As Jack and the reporter, named Sarah, descend the mountain, they discuss their plan of action. Sarah had done a lot of research on the suicides on the mountain, and she had some ideas of where to look for clues.

"The victim's name was Marcus King," Sarah said as they navigated the steep terrain. "He was a local artist who had been battling depression for a long time. His body was found near the summit, just like yours."

Jack nodded, listening intently. "And you think there's more to this than just a simple suicide?"

Sara nodded. "There were a few things that didn't add up. For one thing, Marcus was an experienced hiker. He knew this mountain like the back of his hand, and he wouldn't have made the mistake of falling off the trail. And on his body There were some strange marks that the coroner couldn't explain."

Jack got interested. "What kind of mark?"

"They were like burn marks, but they weren't from a fire. It was almost like they had been branded."

Jack was taken aback, feeling a sense of uneasiness. "It doesn't feel good."

Sara nodded. "That's why I need your help. I think there is something on the mountain that will help us solve this mystery. Something that might have been overlooked by the authorities."

As they descend the mountain, Jack keeps his eyes peeled for any signs of the unusual markings Sarah has described. They searched for hours, climbing up and down the rugged terrain, but found nothing.

Just as they were about to give up, Jack saw something glistening in the sunlight. It was a small, shiny object that got stuck in the rocks. Jack climbed up to take a closer look and saw that it was a metal button with a strange symbol on it.

Sara followed him, and he showed her the button. "What do you make of this?"

Sara took the button and examined it closely. "It is a symbol that was used by a local cult that was active in the area about ten years ago. They were known for their extreme beliefs and dangerous practices. They were eventually shut down by the authorities, but their Some members may still be active."

Jack's heart raced as he realized the implications of what Sarah was saying. "Do you think he had anything to do with Marcus' death?"

Sara nodded seriously. "It's possible. I think we need to investigate this further."

FOUR
Creed Lair

Jack and Sara knew they would have to act quickly. They had discovered the cult's symbol on the mountain, and Sara's research confirmed that the cult had been active in the area years before. They were getting closer to the truth, but they also knew that they were in danger.

The next day, they decide to drive to a nearby town and do some digging. They went to the local library and spent hours digging through old newspapers, trying to find any mention of the cult. They found some articles that confirmed the existence of the cult, but they were short on details.

As they are leaving the library, Sarah receives a call from an unknown source. The man claimed to have knowledge about the cult and wanted to meet them in person.

Jack and Sara agree to the meeting and go to the specified location. It was an abandoned warehouse on the outskirts of town. As he pulled up, he saw a figure standing outside. He was a tall, impressive man in a black cloak and hat. He invited them inside.

As they entered the warehouse, they saw several other clothed figures standing around. They were all wearing the same sign they had found on the mountain.

The leader of the group, a man named Aaron, spoke to them in a low, threatening voice. "What do you want from us?"

Sara strode forward, trying to keep her voice steady. "We are investigating the death of Marcus King. We think you may have a cult connection."

Aaron's face hardened. "We don't know anything about that. And even if we did, we wouldn't tell you. Our ways are not for outsiders."

Jack stepped forward and tried to defuse the situation. "We are not here to cause any trouble. We just want to know the truth. Can you help us?"

Aaron hesitated for a moment, then nodded. "I can show you something that might be interesting. But you must promise to keep it to yourself. If anyone finds out, it could mean the end of our organization."

Jack and Sarah agree to the terms, and Aaron takes them to the warehouse. They went through a series of tunnels and stairs until they reached a hidden room at the bottom of the building.

Inside, he found a collection of books and artifacts. It was clear that this was the lair of the cult. Aaron gave them a book and pointed out a path.

"This is just what you've been looking for. It will tell you everything you need to know about our organization."

Jack and Sara begin reading the passage and their eyes widen in surprise. It describes a ritual involving a human sacrifice on a mountain. The sacrifice was to appease a supernatural entity that the cult worshipped.

As he finished reading, he heard noises outside the room. It felt as if the police had come.

Head to the next chapter: Jack and Sara are trapped in the cult's lair, with the police closing in. They know they have to escape, but they also have to make sure they take the evidence with them. In the next chapter, they will face their toughest challenge yet, as they struggle to stay alive and uncover the truth.

FIVE

THE GREAT STAMPEDE

Jack and Sara stood frozen in terror as they heard the police pounding outside the door. They had just uncovered the cult's lair and the evidence they needed, but now they were trapped and had no way out.

The cult leader, Aaron, looked at him with a sly smile. "It looks like you're in a bind. Perhaps you should join our organization. We could use people with your skills."

Jack nodded. "We're not interested in joining a cult. We just want to get out of here alive."

Aaron laughed. "Good luck with that. The police won't go easy on you, and neither will we if you try to give away our secrets."

Suddenly the door opened and the police came in with guns drawn. Jack and Sara raise their hands, trying to look as innocent as possible.

"Hands behind your back," barked an officer. "You are under arrest on suspicion of trespassing and involvement in the death of Marcus King."

Jack and Sara knew they had to act fast. They looked at each other, silently explaining their plan. They will distract the police, run for it and hope for the best.

As police began to handcuff him, Jack suddenly lunged forward, knocking one officer off balance. Sara followed suit, kicking another officer in the shin.

The feet of Aaron and his followers were burning. They ran through winding tunnels trying to get out. But the cult members were gaining on them, and they knew they had to act fast.

Sara sees a ladder leading up to the trap door. "Jack, up there! We can climb out!"

They climbed up the ladder, emerging on the roof of the building. They could hear the cult members shouting below them, trying to locate them.

"We've got to jump," said Jack, keeping an eye on the edge of the roof. "This is our only chance."

Sara looked at him with horrified eyes. "Are you crazy? We'll break your legs!"

Jack nodded. "We have no choice. Trust me."

He took a deep breath and jumped off the roof, landing on the ground with a thud. Sara followed suit, bracing for effect.

They hit the ground hard and stopped. He looked up, expecting to see the cult members around him. But they were nowhere to be seen.

"We have to go," Jack said, pulling Sara to her feet. "Before they come back."

He ran to his car with his heart thumping with adrenaline. As soon as he left, he knew he had the evidence he needed to bring the cult to justice.

SIX

PIECES OF THE PUZZLE

Jack and Sara sit in their motel room, contemplating the evidence they've gathered from the cult's lair. They had some clues, but nothing that could conclusively link the cult to the death of Marcus King.

"It's crazy," Sara said, running her hand through her hair. "How can we understand all this?"

Jack shrugged. "We just have to keep digging. There must be something we're missing."

He looked at the evidence once more and tried to piece the puzzle together. They had documents outlining the cult's beliefs and practices as well as a list of their members. But there didn't seem to be anything linking them to the death of Marcus King.

Suddenly, Jack's phone rings, jolting him out of his thoughts. It was an unknown number.

"Greetings?" Jack replied.

"Mr. Thompson, I'm Detective Williams. I would like you and Miss Peters to come to the station. We have some questions for you."

Jack's heart sank. They were caught.

"Sure, we'll be there soon," he said, trying to sound normal.

He hung up the phone and turned to Sara. "We have to go to the station. The police want to talk to us."

Sara's face turned white. "what we are going to do?"

Jack put a hand on her shoulder. "We just have to tell the truth. They can't catch us if we haven't done anything wrong."

Their hearts racing, they went to the police station. When they arrived, they were taken to a small room with Detective Williams and another officer.

"Mr. Thompson, Miss Peters," Detective Williams said, eyeing them warily. "We have reason to believe that you were involved in the death of Marcus King, and that you have ties to a dangerous cult."

Jack and Sara exchange bewildered glances. "We have nothing to do with Marcus King's death," Jack said. "We were just trying to investigate a cult that we think may have been involved."

The officer raised an eyebrow. "And how did you come to this conclusion?"

Sara hands over a file of documents, saying, "We found evidence in their lair that suggests they may be involved."

As the officers examine the evidence, their expressions grow more serious. "We'll have to look into this," said Detective Williams. "In the meantime, you are free to go. But don't leave town."

Jack and Sara heave a sigh of relief as they leave the station. He knew that he was getting closer to the truth.

"We have to keep probing," Sara said, determination in her voice. "We can't let them get away with it."

Jack nodded. "Agreed. But we have to be careful. They're on us now."

SEVEN

Ex Follower

Jack and Sara move to a small town in the middle of nowhere. They had received a tip from an anonymous source that one of the former cult members was living there, and may have information about Marcus King's death.

He parked outside a dilapidated house and knocked on the door. A middle-aged man with a scruffy beard replied.

"Can I help you?" she asked suspiciously.

"We're looking for a man named Thomas," said Jack. "We heard that he used to be part of a cult that we are investigating."

The man's face hardened. "I don't know what you're talking about," she said, starting to close the door.

"Wait," said Sara, folding her hands. "We're not here to cause trouble. We just want to talk to Thomas. We think he can help us."

The man heaved a sigh and opened the door. "Okay. He's back. But I don't know if he'll talk to you."

They followed him through the house and into a small room in the back. A thin, nervous man was sitting in a chair, staring at the wall.

"Thomas?" Sara said softly.

He turned to look at them, his eyes brimming with panic. "Who are you?"

"We're investigating the cult you used to be a part of," Jack said. "We think they may have been involved in a murder, and we're trying to get to the bottom of it."

Thomas shifted in his chair, clearly uncomfortable. "I don't know anything about murder."

"We understand you left the cult," Sara said. "We're hoping you can tell us what you know about their practices and beliefs."

Thomas looked around nervously. "I don't want to talk about it," he said. "If I do they will follow me."

"We can protect you," said Jack. "But we need your help. If you know anything, anything, it could make a difference."

Thomas hesitated, then began to speak. He told them about the rituals of the cult, the way they isolated themselves from the outside world, and their extreme beliefs.

"They thought they were doing the right thing," Thomas said, his voice trembling. "But they were so twisted. I had to get out of there."

Jack and Sara listened carefully, taking notes. He was finally getting the information he needed to bring the cult to justice.

As they were leaving, Jack turned to Thomas. "Thank you. You've been a great help. But you need to know that the cult will come after you if they find out you talked to us."

Thomas nodded. "I know. But I can't live in fear. I have to do what's right."

EIGHT

HUNT FOR CULT LEADER

Jack and Sara meet Detective Rodriguez at a local diner. He shares information gathered from his own investigation and from Thomas, a former member of the cult.

"That's good stuff," Rodriguez said, scanning his notes. "But we still need to find the leader. He's the key to this whole thing."

"I think I may know where he is," said Sara. "Thomas mentioned a compound in the mountains. It's isolated, and they may be hiding out there."

Rodriguez frowned. "It's a big area to search. But we don't have much choice. We have to find this man before he does any more damage."

He spent the next few days combing the mountains, searching for any sign of the cult's compound. It was slow going, and they encountered many obstacles along the way. But eventually, they stumble upon a small cabin in a clearing.

As they approached, they heard chanting from inside. They drew their weapons and moved closer, trying to hide.

"I'll go in first," whispered Rodriguez. "You two follow me, but stay back until I give the signal."

He pushed open the door and slipped inside. Jack and Sarah follow behind, keeping a safe distance.

The room was dimly lit and the walls were lined with candles. In the center of the room, a man in a black robe was leading the chant. They couldn't see his face, but they knew he was the leader of the cult.

Rodriguez signals them to go inside. They approached the cult leader from all sides, their guns drawn.

"Freeze!" Rodriguez shouted.

The cult leader turned and faced them. "You're too late," he said. "The sacrifice has already been made."

Suddenly a loud bang shook the room. The cult leader slumps in the chaos, and they scramble for cover.

"What the hell was that?" Rodriguez screamed at the noise.

Jack looked around nervously. "The cabin is bound to explode!" He shouted.

They ran for the door, but debris had started falling from the ceiling. They get out just in time as the cabin collapses in a heap of flames.

As he caught his breath, Rodriguez turned to him. "We lost him," he said. "But at least we know he's still out there. And we have a pretty good idea of what he's capable of."

NINE

SECRETS REVEALED

Jack, Sara and Detective Rodriguez track down several former cult members. After some persuasion, he finally found someone who was willing to talk. A woman named Rachel left the cult many years ago and has been trying to start a new life ever since.

"I don't know where they are now," Rachel said, her eyes darting around the room nervously. "But I can tell you what they were planning."

"Go," Rodriguez urged.

"They were building an army," said Rachel. "They believed the world was ending, and they were preparing for the end times. They had weapons, explosives, everything you can imagine."

"What was his endgame?" Sara asked.

"They wanted to take over the world," Rachel replied. "They believed that they were the only ones who could save humanity. But the only way to do so was to destroy everything else."

Jack felt a chill run down his spine. The cult leader was much more dangerous than they thought. "Do you know where they were getting their weapons?" He asked.

Rachel nodded. "They were very secretive about it. But I know they had a lot of money. They could have bought them from anybody."

Rodriguez wrote notes in his notebook. "We will need to track down their financial records," he said. "If we can trace where the money was coming from, we might be able to trace it to their suppliers."

He thanks Rachel for her help and leaves her to her own devices. As they walk back to their car, Jack can't help but feel like he's getting closer to the truth.

"We need to find his financial records," he said. "This is our next step."

Sara said, "We need to know more about this end-times scenario they're planning." "If we can figure out what they're preparing for, we might be able to predict their next move."

Rodriguez nodded in agreement. "We'll hit the financial records first. Then we'll see what else we can uncover."

TEN

UNVEILED THE TRUTH

Jack, Sara and Rodriguez spend the next few days digging through the cult's financial records. He traced the money back to a series of shell companies and fake charities, all designed to conceal the true source of his funds. But eventually, they were able to track it back to a wealthy merchant named George Tipton.

"Tipton had been on our radar for some time," Rodriguez said while looking through the documents. "We suspected that he was involved in some suspicious transactions, but we could never prove it."

"What's that got to do with the cult?" Sara asked.

Rodriguez replied, "That's what we need to find out." "We need to bring him in for questioning."

Jack nodded. "I'll have a meeting with him. He must not be expecting me."

The meeting was scheduled for the next day at a coffee shop in the heart of the city. Jack arrived early, and he was surprised to find that Tipton was already waiting for him.

"Mr. Ryder," said Tipton, rising from his seat. "To what do I owe this happiness?"

"I think you know why I'm here," said Jack, taking a seat in front of her. "We've been looking through your financial records, and we've found some interesting connections to a certain cult.

"Tipton's face remained fixed. "I'm not sure what you're talking about," he said.

"Don't be silly, Tipton," said Jack. "We know you're funding the cult. We just want to know why."

Tipton sighed. "Okay. I'll tell you what I find out. But you have to promise to keep me out of this."

"Depends on what you tell us," said Jack.

Tipton bent down, his voice low. "The cult was just a front. They were working for a much larger organization, which has been operating in secret for years. They call themselves the 'New World Order', and their goal is to create a one-world government." , with himself on top."

Jack felt a chill run down his spine. "And you're helping them?"

Tipton nodded. "I didn't know what I was getting into at first. They approached me with an offer I couldn't refuse. But as I went deeper into it, I realized what they were planning. I thought it was a way to keep them under control. But I was wrong."

"What are they planning?" Sara asked.

"I don't know the details," Tipton said. "But I know they're getting ready to make their move. They're going to attack soon, and when they do, it's going to be chaos. They believe only they can save the world." But really, they're going to destroy it."

Jack stood up, his mind racing. "We need to stop them. Now."

ELEVEN

LAST SHOWDOWN

Jack, Sara, and Rodriguez work around the clock, poring over documents, following leads, and gathering intelligence on the New World Order. They knew that time was running out, and they were determined to stop the organization before it was too late.

After many sleepless nights, he finally had a breakthrough. They had located the headquarters of the New World Order, a heavily fortified complex in the heart of the city.

"We have to move fast," said Jack as they gathered in his office. "They're going to attack soon, and we can't let that happen."

"We have a problem," Sarah said, her tone strained. "The compound is heavily guarded. We can never get in without a fight."

"We have to take that risk," Rodriguez said. "We can't let them succeed."

Jack nodded. "We're going to need a plan. We can't blindly charge out there."

They spent the next few hours strategizing, considering every possible scenario and contingency plan. Finally, he had a plan that he was confident would work.

The next morning, they arrive at the compound, ready for battle. They brought a team of highly trained agents, and they were equipped with the latest weapons and equipment.

As they approached the compound, they were met with a volley of gunfire. The New World Order was waiting for them, and they were ready.

The fighting was fierce and intense, with both sides suffering heavy losses. But Jack, Sara and Rodriguez were determined to see it through to the end.

Finally, they breached the inner sanctum of the compound, where they found the leader of the New World Order, a shadowy figure known only as "the Architect".

The architect was a middle-aged man, with a thin face and cold, calculating eyes. He looked up as Jack and his team entered the room, the hint of a smile on his lips.

"Good, good, good," she said, her voice as smooth as silk. "I was wondering when you would show up."

"We're here to stop you," Jack said, his voice stern.

The architect laughed. "And how do you plan to do that? You cannot stop progress, Agent Rider. The New World Order is the future."

"Not if we have anything to say about it," Sara said in a steely voice.

The architect shook his head. "You're too late. The plan is already in motion. There's nothing you can do to stop it."

"We'll see about that," said Rodriguez, his eyes gleaming with anger.

The architect smiled. "You are welcome to try. But I warn you, the consequences will be dire."

And with that, he pressed a button on his desk, which caused a massive explosion that shook the entire building.

Jack, Sara and Rodriguez are thrown to the ground, their ears ringing with the sound of the explosion. When he looked up, he saw that the architect had disappeared, leaving behind nothing but rubble and smoke.

TWELVE

FINAL CLIMB

The team rose early the next day, determined to complete their mission. They had a long day and the weather was against them. The wind was picking up, and it was getting colder by the minute. Nevertheless, they set out for the summit with determination.

As they climbed higher, the wind picked up and the temperature dropped drastically. The team had to stop to rest and catch their breath, and they were beginning to worry that they would not reach the summit before nightfall.

"I'm not sure we can go on like this," Rachel said tremblingly. "It's too dangerous. We must turn back."

"We can't hold back now," James said firmly. "We're almost there. We have to keep going."

The team moved slowly but steadily and after several hours they finally reached the summit. The feeling of accomplishment was overwhelming, but it was short-lived.

When he looked around, he noticed something strange. There were no bodies. They had climbed all this way, battled the elements, risked their lives, and had nothing to show for it.

"I don't understand," Maria said confusedly. "It doesn't make any sense. There must be corpses here."

James felt a pit in his stomach. Something was not right. "We need to search the area. Maybe they fell through a crack or something."

The team searched the area for any trace of the missing bodies. After several minutes of tension, he heard a scream.

"Over here! I found something!"

They reached the source of the call, and there, in a small crevice, were the missing bodies.

James felt a sense of relief and horror. He was relieved that they had found the bodies, but was horrified to see them. They were frozen, twisted in awkward positions, their faces contorted in agony. It was clear that he had suffered a lot before he died.

"We need to bring them down," James said grimly. "We can't leave them here like this."

The team acted quickly, secured the bodies and carefully carried them down the mountain. The descent was treacherous, but they made it to the bottom safely.

As he loaded the bodies onto the transport vehicle, James could not help but feel a sense of sadness and loss. He had seen many bodies in his field of work, but this one was different. They were not just victims of suicide, but victims of something greater. He couldn't shake the feeling that there was more to this story than they knew.

As the team heads away from the mountain, James resolves to find out by himself what really happened there, no matter what.

THIRTEEN

SOLVE THE MYSTERY

Tired and shaken from their journey up the mountain, the team returned to their base camp. James could not shake the feeling that something was not quite right about the suicides he had recovered. He stayed up all night rummaging through the case files, looking for any clue that might shed light on what had happened.

The next day, James and Rachel go to the local police station to see if they can get any additional information about the suicides. They met with a detective who had worked on the cases and shared their suspicions that there may be more to the story.

The detective was hesitant to share too much information, but did reveal that a cult was rumored to operate in the area. The cult is believed to have persuaded individuals to climb to the top of the mountain and jump, promising them a better afterlife if they did so.

James and Rachel are stunned. He had heard of cults before, but had never encountered them in his field of work. He knew he needed to know more.

He began by looking at the background of individuals who committed suicide. They found that many of them were battling depression and other mental health problems. It seemed that the cult preyed on these vulnerabilities in order to recruit new members.

James and Rachel continue to dig, interviewing local people and gathering information about the cult. They learned that it was being led by a charismatic figure who claimed to have special powers and knowledge about the afterlife. He persuaded many people to follow him by promising them a better life after death.

As they delved deeper, James and Rachel realized that the cult was still active, and that they were recruiting new members. They knew they would have to act fast to stop them.

The team organizes a sting operation, working with local police, to track down the cult leader and his followers. He fakes a suicide jump to lure the cult members to the top of the mountain. When they arrived, they were met by James and the team, who were hiding nearby.

"Stop there," said James, stepping forward. "you're under arrest."

The cult members were stunned, but the leader remained defiant. "You can't stop us," he said. "We have the power to control our own destiny."

James nodded. "No one has the power to control our own destiny. We all have a choice, and we choose to live."

The team apprehends the cult members and turns them over to the authorities. They knew that they had saved countless lives by preventing the cult from preying on vulnerable individuals.

As he left the mountain for the last time, James could not help but feel a sense of satisfaction. Not only did they recover the bodies of suicide victims, but they also helped prevent future tragedies. It was a small victory in the grand scheme of things, but it was a victory nonetheless.

FOURTEEN

Moving On

James and Rachel return to their offices, their work on the mountain finally done. They were both physically and emotionally exhausted after their time on the mountain, but they felt satisfied with the result.

As they sat in his office, completing paperwork, Rachel turned to James. "You know," she said, "I'm really glad we were able to stop that cult. It feels like we really made a difference."

James nodded. "Yeah, it does. But I can't help but feel like there's always going to be more, you know? More people who need our help, more mysteries to solve."

Rachel smiled. "That's what we're here for, James. To help people and solve mysteries. It's our job, but it's also what we're good at."

They worked in silence for a few more minutes before Rachel spoke again. "Hey, do you remember when we first started working together?"

James laughed. "How could I forget? You were so green then. I had to show you the ropes."

Rachel rolled her eyes. "I wasn't that green. And I remember teaching you a thing or two."

James smiled. "Yeah, you did. You've always been good at thinking outside the box, and I've learned a lot from you over the years."

Rachel smiled back at him. "You know, we make a really good team. Maybe we should stick together a while."

James smiled. "That's what I was thinking too. Besides, I don't know if I can work with anyone else."

They both laughed and continued to work, the clicks of their keyboards filling the room. They had been through a lot together over the years, and they both knew that they would be there for each other no matter what.

As the day wore on, he finished his work and packed up to go home. They walked out of the office together, the sun shining. As they left, Rachel turned to James.

"So what do you say we have drinks to celebrate a job well done?"

James smiled. "I say it's a good idea."

They stood by the side of the road, shoulder to shoulder, ready for whatever mystery or challenge might come their way. For James and Rachel, the adventure never really ended, and they wouldn't have it any other way.

FIFTEEN

ENDING

Several months had passed since James and Rachel had been on the mountain, and life had settled into a routine again. He had taken on new cases and solved new mysteries, but the events at the mountain were still on his mind.

One day, James receives a call from the local police department. They were informed of a hiker missing in the area, and needed James and Rachel's help to find her.

As they pass through the mountains, James and Rachel talk about their past experience on the mountain. "It's hard to believe it's been months since we've been there," Rachel said.

James nodded. "Yeah, it seems like a lifetime ago. But we were able to help a lot of people out there, and that's what counts."

As they went on, they saw something in the distance. As they got closer, they realized it was the body of the missing hiker.

As they worked to recover the bodies, James couldn't help but think about the suicides they had recovered on the mountain. He said to Rachel, "It looks like this place is cursed."

Rachel nodded. "It's certainly terrible, but we can't let it get to us. We have a job to do."

As they finish their work, James and Rachel take a moment to reflect on the events that have brought them to this point. "It's strange," said James. "When we were on the mountain, it seemed like there was no end to the darkness. But now, looking back, I can see that there was a light at the end of the tunnel."

Rachel smiled. "That's the thing about our work. We may be dealing with some of the darkest parts of humanity, but we're always working toward a better outcome. And even though we can't save everyone, we can at least save them." Can shut down."

As they descended the mountain, James and Rachel felt a sense of peace knowing that they had helped another family find closure. They knew there would always be more mysteries to solve and more darkness to confront, but they were ready for whatever came their way.

They walked back to their car in silence, their footsteps echoing through the mountains. As they got in the car and drove off, James and Rachel knew they had done their job well, and that's all that mattered.

9 798889 867586

Printed by Libri Plureos GmbH in Hamburg, Germany